RAINFOREST RESCUE

J. BURCHETT & S. VOGLER

STONE ARCH BOOKS
a capstone imprint

Wild Rescue books are published by Stone Arch Books
A Capstone Imprint
1710 Roe Crest Drive,
North Mankato, Minnesota 56003
www.capstonepub.com

First published by Stripes Publishing Ltd.
1 The Coda Centre
189 Munster Road
London SW6 6AW
© Jan Burchett and Sara Vogler, 2012
Interior art © Diane Le Feyer of Cartoon Saloon, 2012

Library of Congress Cataloging-in-Publication Data
Burchett, Jan.
[Forest fire]
Rainforest rescue / written by Jan Burchett [and] Sara Vogler ; illustrated by
Diane Le Feyer ; cover illustration by Sam Kennedy.
p. cm. -- (Wild rescue)
Originally published under the title Forest fire: London : Stripes, 2009.
ISBN 978-1-4342-3768-2 (library binding)
1. Twins--Juvenile fiction. 2. Brothers and sisters--Juvenile fiction. 3.
Orangutan--Borneo--Juvenile fiction. 4. Wildlife refuges--Borneo--Juvenile fiction.
5. Logging--Borneo--Juvenile fiction. 6. Borneo--Juvenile fiction. 7. Adventure
stories. [1. Twins--Fiction. 2. Brothers and sisters--Fiction. 3. Orangutan--Fiction.
4. Wildlife refuges--Fiction. 5. Logging--Fiction. 6. Borneo--Fiction. 7. Adventure
and adventurers--Fiction.] I. Vogler, Sara. II. Le Feyer, Diane, ill. III. Kennedy,
Sam, 1971- ill. IV. Title.
PZ7.B915966Fo 2012
823.914--dc23   2011025561

Cover Art: Sam Kennedy
Graphic Designer: Russell Griesmer
Production Specialist: Michelle Biedscheid

Design Credits: Shutterstock 51686107 (p. 4-5),
Shutterstock 51614464 (p. 148-149, 150, 152)

Printed in the United States of America in North Mankato, Minnesota.
062012
006809R

TABLE OF CONTENTS

WILDRESCUE

MISSION

BEN WOODWARD
WILD Operative

ZOE WOODWARD
WILD Operative

BRIEFING

TARGET: ◎

CODE NAME: KAWAN

CHAPTER 1
WILD RIDE

Ben pointed at the huge wave rolling toward him and his twin sister, Zoe. "Ready?" he yelled.

Zoe grinned. "Ready!" Lying flat on her surfboard, she began to paddle with her hands. She built up speed as the swell approached. When they felt the wave lift them up, they took it. Together, they sailed toward the shore, arms outstretched. They were having a great week staying at Grandma's cabin by the ocean.

"Awesome," exclaimed Ben. "I felt like a killer shark out there!"

Zoe looked at Ben. He was wearing his shiny brown wetsuit, and his brown hair was sticking up in chaotic spikes. "More like a killer starfish!" she said.

A voice came from behind them. "Ben! Zoe!"

They looked up the beach. Grandma was waving at them and pointing out to sea. They turned to see a sleek speedboat slicing through the water toward them with a familiar blond woman at the helm.

Ben and Zoe watched the speedboat slide to a sudden stop, splashing water into the air. "It's Erika!" Ben said. "Looks like we're off on another WILD adventure!"

Ben and Zoe's parents were international veterinarians. Wherever their work took them, Ben and Zoe usually went. But in a month the two would be starting school, so they had to stay with their grandma for the summer. They'd been expecting three boring months with their grandma until their uncle, Dr. Stephen Fisher, got in touch with them. He recruited them into WILD, his top-secret organization that was dedicated to saving endangered animals. Their grandma knew all about it — but almost no one else did.

After yelling goodbye to Grandma, Ben and Zoe swam out to the speedboat. Erika, Uncle Stephen's second-in-command, stretched out a hand and helped them climb up the ladder.

"It's good to see you again," Erika said as they sped across the waves. "Your uncle is impressed by the work you've done so far with WILD." Erika's expression grew serious. "But this mission's going to be a little different. He's trusting you with a very difficult task. As usual, he wants to tell you the details himself."

Erika handed Zoe an envelope. "Here," she said.

Zoe opened the envelope and tipped it upside down. A glass eyeball fell into her hand. She showed it to Ben.

Ben inspected it closely. "It looks like a human eye," he said. "But the outside part's darker."

Zoe peered at it. "Do you think it's one of the apes?" she asked. "That would be so cool."

Ben knew what to do next. He looked at the speedboat's dashboard and found a small hole next to the radar screen. "Let's find out," he said, slipping the eyeball in.

A hologram of their uncle appeared before them. He wore a baseball cap over his thick red hair and his shirt was hanging out. "Greetings, children!" he said.

Zoe giggled. "He's as weird as ever," she said.

"Ready for an urgent WILD mission?" Stephen asked. Then he chuckled. "I don't know why I'm even asking — of course you are! You two are always up for a challenge. There's an orangutan in trouble in Borneo. I'll tell you more when you get to HQ."

Uncle Stephen gave a cheery wave. The hologram disappeared.

Zoe smiled. "An orangutan!" she said. "They're such interesting, gentle creatures."

"And endangered," Ben added. "Did you know that —"

"Their habitat is threatened by logging?" Zoe asked, cutting her brother off.

"Actually, I was going to say —" Ben began.

"That they can use sign language?" Zoe said. "I knew that, too."

"Let me finish," Ben said, smirking. "I was about to say that they're more intelligent than you are!" Ben ducked away to avoid a playful punch on the shoulder.

Zoe grinned. "Real funny," she said.

* * *

Ben and Zoe saw a small island come into view. As they got closer, they saw a few buildings scattered around a ramshackle farm. Chickens pecked the scrubby land.

As they approached the shore, Erika brought down the sail and steered the speedboat toward a strange-looking dock. As they climbed the waiting ladder, Erika pressed a button on a remote and the boat glided forward into a shed hidden in the bank.

They walked to a nearby outhouse, Erika following them. Ben locked the door behind them and Zoe flushed the toilet. WHOOSH! The cubicle turned into an elevator and descended deep into the earth.

"Who needs an elevator when you have a turbo toilet!" Ben said, laughing.

Moments later, Zoe and Erika followed Ben along a brightly lit hall leading to the Control Room. They placed their fingertips on an ID scanner.

"Print identification complete," announced an electronic voice.

They dashed into a bright room filled with flashing control panels and computer screens. A pair of sandaled feet were sticking out from under a console.

"Uncle Stephen!" Zoe said excitedly.

There was a thump and a muffled voice. Then the tall, thin figure of their uncle emerged, rubbing his head.

"Hello there," he said cheerfully. "Just fixing the computer. I've got the whole place running on solar power now." He looked at their wetsuits. "I know you're going to the rainforest, but it won't be that wet!"

"I picked up Ben and Zoe from the beach," explained Erika.

Uncle Stephen grinned. "Let me tell you about your mission," he said. He touched a screen, bringing up a satellite map of a large island. "Borneo," he said, pointing. "There was once a huge rainforest there, but it's shrunk a lot due to logging — both legal and illegal."

"I've read all about that," said Ben. "They're clearing the land for oil palm plantations. Palm oil is used all over the world, in margarine, soap, candles, makeup — tons of stuff."

"Mr. Know-it-all," Zoe said, rolling her eyes. "But you're right. The rainforest's disappearing really fast. Is that something to do with the orangutan in danger?"

"Exactly, Zoe," said Uncle Stephen. "We've had reports from one of our operatives about an orangutan named Kawan. Until recently, he was living safely on the Adilah Reservation. But then he suddenly disappeared."

"Mat Ginting, who runs the reservation, had raised him since the ape was a baby," Erika explained. "He reintroduced Kawan into the wild just last year."

"Orangutans don't become independent until they're about seven or eight, do they?" said Ben. "No other animal in the world stays with its mother that long."

"You're correct, Ben," said Uncle Stephen. "Kawan's about eight now. He adapted well to living in the wild and had established his own territory. Male orangutans live alone and their territory is very important to them. The only time they come near other orangutans is for mating or to fight another male who trespassed into their space."

"But just two weeks ago, there was some illegal logging in his area," said Erika. "Some men came at night and cut down several trees before they were chased away. They intended to steal lumber and then sell it. One of the chopped-down trees had an orangutan nest made of leaves that must've been Kawan's. He fled in terror and hasn't been back since."

"So he completely vanished?" asked Zoe.

"There have been a couple of sightings outside the reservation on a nearby oil palm plantation," Uncle Stephen said. "But he hasn't wanted to come back to his territory. Kawan is essential for Mr. Ginting's dream of increasing the orangutan population. There are very few males on the reservation and he's needed to mate with the females."

"And orangutans breed very slowly, don't they?" said Ben.

Uncle Stephen nodded. "A female may only have two or three babies in her whole lifetime." He pressed a button on the screen again and a photo of a smiling young man with black hair appeared. "This is Mat Ginting. He set up the reservation ten years ago to help preserve the rainforest and its endangered inhabitants."

"He must be very brave," said Zoe. "I read that there are a lot of people who'll do anything to get control of rainforest land."

"Indeed, Zoe," agreed Uncle Stephen. "Mat's one in a million. He's been running the reservation against all the odds, but money's becoming increasingly tight, so he's going to start taking paying visitors."

"Apparently there's a grand opening in a few days," Erika added, "which is perfect timing for us. Tourists will be able to stay there and see orangutans in their natural habitat."

"So you want us to pose as visitors to the reservation, locate Kawan, and bring him back to his home?" asked Ben.

Uncle Stephen nodded. "Of course, Mat Ginting can't know about our organization," he said. "And that's why you two are perfect for the job. He won't suspect a couple of kids."

"We're pretending you've won a competition by writing about endangered wildlife," said Erika.

"Erika's idea," Uncle Stephen said proudly. "And a very good one."

"We've told Mr. Ginting that the prize was a trip to a sanctuary in Brunei," Erika said, "but unfortunately the people there had to cancel at the last minute due to illness. We asked if he could take you instead. He was delighted. In fact, you're going to be his very first guests."

"So you need to be on your way," said Uncle Stephen. "Right away!"

"What about our BUGs?" Ben reminded him.

"Of course!" Their uncle handed them what looked like two video game consoles. The Brilliant Undercover Gizmos performed many useful functions. They had communicators, scent dispersers, translators, and much more.

"I invented a new gadget especially for this mission," said Uncle Stephen.

Their uncle handed Ben and Zoe two belts and two pairs of boots. "Inside the boots there is an EEL — the Electronic Escape Line," Uncle Stephen said. "It's a top-of-the-line bungee cord that might come in handy."

"In other words, it will save your life if you're falling from great heights!" said Erika. "You'll be spending some time in the trees in Borneo. All you need to do to activate it is press the silver button on the belt." She demonstrated how to use the device.

Uncle Stephen ducked under the console again. "Erika will take you where you need to go," he called out. "Hope you get Kawan back!"

"You can count on us!" Ben said.

CHAPTER 2

THE RESERVATION

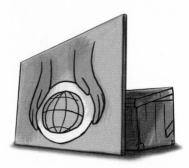

Erika drove a rental jeep through a pair of wooden gates. She parked in a dirt patch next to some new wooden buildings. "The Adilah Reservation," she said. "We're here!"

The buildings around them formed a big square courtyard. There were colorful flags and banners everywhere. Trees lined one side of the courtyard, as if the rainforest was trying to take back this little space. Ben and Zoe jumped out of the car and gasped as the humidity and heat hit them in the face.

After spending so much time in the cool of the car's air-conditioning, the change in temperature was shocking. Insects buzzed overhead. They could hear exotic bird and animal cries coming from the forest.

Ben swiveled his head and looked around. He saw two workers fixing a banner over the entrance of one of the buildings. It read: "Grand Opening Today".

One of the nearby men came over to greet them. He was carrying a hammer, nails, and a heavy sign. Ben and Zoe recognized him from the photo their uncle had shown them.

"Hello there! You must be Ben and Zoe!" He put down his tools and sign and shook their hands enthusiastically. "I'm Mat Ginting. Welcome to my reservation."

"We're so excited to be here," said Zoe.

Erika took out their backpacks from the jeep's trunk. "We're so thankful you agreed to take on our winners," she said to Mat. "I'll pick them up later." She waved goodbye. "Enjoy your prize, Ben and Zoe."

"Thank you, Ms. Bohn," they replied politely. The children knew they had to hide how well they knew her. It had to seem like she was simply the organizer of the competition — not heading north to check out reports of more illegal logging.

Zoe looked at the sign Mat had been carrying. It showed a huge O encircling a globe, supported by caring hands. On the way to the reservation, they'd passed field after field where the forest had been cleared for oil palm trees. Every one of them had the sign displayed.

"Whose logo is that?" asked Zoe. "We saw it several times on the way here."

"Ostriander Industries," Mat told her. "Peter Ostriander, the owner, has generously given us donations to help our work. The least we could do is put up his plantation logo in time for the ceremony. He's promised to give a speech."

"But isn't his plantation threatening the rainforest?" asked Ben. "It's taken over a huge area. We drove for several miles seeing nothing but his oil palms."

"And they're not even a native tree of Borneo," added Zoe.

"We have to keep a balance," said Mat. "The plantation gives jobs to the locals, but we also have to preserve the forest. That's why I bought this land and why I'll keep it safe. When Peter first bought the plantation a few years ago, he approached me and asked if I would sell him my reservation."

Mat smiled warmly. "When I told Mr. Ostriander what I was doing, he became very supportive," Mat said. "In fact, I recently had some trouble with illegal logging in the eastern part of my land. Peter lent me some men to patrol the area and the loggers haven't been back since. Peter has been a good friend to our cause."

"Greetings!" called a voice.

A smiling young woman emerged from one of the buildings. A baby orangutan clung to her neck, its head resting against her shoulder. It had soft orange hair and a round, fuzzy belly. It smiled at the children.

"My name is Yasmin," said the woman. She pushed her long, dark bangs out of her eyes. "I am Mat's wife. You must be the competition winners. Congratulations."

"Thank you," Ben said with a grin.

"Who's this?" asked Zoe. She stroked the soft fur of the baby orangutan. It grabbed her finger and held it like a baby might. Zoe let out a happy sigh.

"His name is Biza," said Yasmin. "He is an orphan we are taking care of. They go back into the wild when they are old enough."

"But they do come back to see us," added Mat. "Orangutans make a bond with their primary caregivers. Some of the females show us their babies as if we were their grandparents!"

"And we are just as proud," said Yasmin, smiling. "Come with me. Biza and I will show you your bedroom so you can unpack. Our opening ceremony is one hour from now."

Ben and Zoe followed her through a kitchen with a huge table and into a hallway lined with bedrooms.

"These are the guest rooms," Yasmin said. "Mat will be waiting for you in his office across the courtyard. When you're ready, head on over." She smiled, waved, and quickly left.

The room was cool and comfortable. It had two beds and a bathroom. Ben and Zoe quickly emptied their backpacks, leaving only their important WILD gear.

Zoe detached the translator earpiece from her BUG and stuck it into her ear. "Don't forget yours, Ben," she said, pointing to her ear. "We have to understand everything that people are saying when they speak Malay."

The children found Mat sitting in an office, working at an old-fashioned computer. "I'm updating my records while I have a chance," he told them as they entered. "I make daily entries about all our orangutans . . . well, all of them but one."

"Why not all?" Zoe said, acting as if she had no idea who Kawan was.

Ben grinned. His sister wasn't wasting time getting some intel for their mission.

"One of our orangutans has left the reservation," Mat told them. He frowned. "He's a young male called Kawan and he was with us since he was tiny. Some poachers took him from his mother and were going to sell him as a pet to some rich collector!"

"That's awful!" said Zoe.

"Luckily, they were arrested, and Kawan was brought to me," Mat said. "I couldn't find his mother, so I had to raise him myself. He was the first orangutan I took in."

Mat sighed. He was obviously sad. "I released him into the wild last year," he said, "but he still visited me every morning for a snack. That is, until two weeks ago, when the logging scared him away."

"Maybe he's scared of humans because of what happened when he was little," Ben said.

"It seems that way," Mat said sadly. "At least I know he's alive. One of my staff, Daud, saw him on Mr. Ostriander's oil palm plantation at the edge of the reservation a little while ago."

Mat's smile returened. "Say, would you like to see some footage of Kawan doing his jungle training?" he asked. "It's me showing him how to look after himself. I'm sure we have time before the ceremony."

"Yes, please!" said Ben and Zoe together.

Mat took them into a large room where log benches faced a screen. He gestured for them to sit. "You're the first guests to see this," he said. "Daud filmed it. He's very fond of Kawan, too."

The screen flashed to life. The words "Adilah Reservation" appeared. Mat fast-forwarded to a scene where he was teaching a tiny orangutan how to climb a tree. The solemn little ape had an adorable tuft of hair sticking up on one side of his head. He was diligently copying every move until Mat made a strange chirping noise.

"Kawan always comes to that call," explained Mat. "Now he must be too far away to hear it. When the grand opening is over, I'm going to go and find him. Peter let me look on the plantation before, but I haven't had the chance to do a thorough search. The plantation's not a natural home for an orangutan, so he's probably eating the young oil palm seedlings. That's not fair to Peter."

They watched the footage of young Kawan responding to Mat's call. He stopped his task, climbed on Mat's head, and clung to his ears.

"Aww," said Ben. "That's pretty cute. Can we watch it again?"

Zoe shot Ben a puzzled look. It wasn't like her brother to get excited about animals. That was her thing.

But as the film replayed she saw him pull out his BUG and hit a button on it. Now she knew what he was up to. He was recording Mat's call! She smiled. If they could get to Kawan's old territory, they could play the recording through the megaphone on the BUG. Hopefully the orangutan would hear it and come home.

CHAPTER 3

GRAND OPENING

Ben looked out the window at the courtyard. He stared hungrily at the feast spread out on tables. "Look at all that food!" he said. "I'm ready for my lunch."

"You'll have to wait until after the speeches," whispered Zoe. "The opening ceremony is about to begin."

Ben and Zoe were standing with Mat, Yasmin, and Biza at the front of a large crowd of people. A reporter was already taking photos of the new buildings.

Everyone was waiting for Peter Ostriander to arrive. One of the workers was putting coolers filled with drinks on the table. He saw Ben staring at the food and smiled. The worker handed him a hunk of bread.

Ben tore into it. "Thanks!" he said, his mouth full. "I'm sorry, I don't know your name."

"I'm Daud," said the young man. He pointed to anther man with gray hair. "And that is Talib. We both work for Mat."

Ben and Zoe started to introduce themselves when the roar of an engine cut them off. A sleek, sporty jeep drove through the gates. Something large was in the back, wrapped in brown paper. The jeep came to a stop. A tall, tanned man in expensive clothes stepped out. He smiled widely at everyone and waved.

Mat waved at Mr. Ostriander. "Come and meet our competition winners, Peter," he said as Peter approached. "This is Ben and Zoe, Mr. Ostriander."

"I've heard all about you," Peter said. "Well done! So what do you think made your entry the best one?"

Zoe saw Ben's eyes glance at her. They both realized they didn't have a cover story.

Zoe hesitated. "We, um, wrote an essay on . . ." she began.

"The problems facing the giant panda in the wild," Ben said, finishing Zoe's sentence.

That was smart, thought Zoe. They both knew a lot about pandas, since they'd saved one themselves not too long ago.

"Fascinating," said Mr. Ostriander. "It's good to see young people like you taking such an interest in endangered species."

"Mat has told us all about you, too, Mr. Ostriander," said Ben. "He explained how much your company has helped him with the reservation."

"Just doing my small part to help a greater cause," Mr. Ostriander said. "We both want the same thing — to protect our natural resources."

"I think we're ready now, Peter," said Mat. He nodded at Mr. Ostriander, then they both turned to face the crowd.

Mat began to speak in Malay. Luckily, Ben and Zoe's earpieces were translating every word. "Thank you for coming here today for the Grand Opening Ceremony of the Adilah Reservation!" he said loudly. "Mr. Ostriander will now say a few words."

Mr. Ostriander smiled at the assembled crowd. "We are here today to open this wonderful place," he said. "I would like to say a few words to honor the man who made it all possible — Mat Ginting."

Mat bent his head and blushed as Mr. Ostriander spoke favorably about him, thanking Mat for all the hard work he had done. He complimented the staff, then thanked everyone for coming.

"In conclusion," Mr. Ostriander said, ending his speech, "I declare the Adilah Reservation open for business." He walked over to his jeep. "Now if your men could give me a hand, I have a present for the reservation."

Mat spoke over his shoulder in Malay. Talib and Daud walked over to the jeep. They helped Mr. Ostriander lift out the large, bulky package and set it on the ground. It looked like it was very heavy.

Mr. Ostriander cut the string and pulled away the paper. Everyone gasped as the wooden statue of an orangutan was revealed. The reporter stepped forward and took pictures.

"It's amazing!" Mat said, admiring the hand carved wood. "It will look wonderful next to the main gate."

Yasmin pointed at the tables. "Now dig in, everyone!" she cried.

Ben didn't wait to be asked twice. As Ben and Zoe piled their plates with food, Mat came over. "When the event is over, I'll give you a tour of the reservation," he said.

"Awesome!" Ben said. Zoe shot him a knowing glance. Each of the twins knew what the other was thinking — they would both ask Mat to take them to Kawan's old territory to look for clues.

CHAPTER 4

A PRIVATE TOUR

The ceremony and meal were over at last, and Ben and Zoe sat in the shade of the reservation courtyard. Ben fidgeted impatiently.

"Sit still!" Zoe poked her brother in the ribs. "Mat said he'd be here right after he said goodbye to all his guests."

"I know, but I'm too excited," Ben said. He stood and glanced at the map displayed on the wall behind them. "A guided tour on walkways right up in the trees. So cool!"

"Don't forget, we're here for Kawan," Zoe reminded him. "We have to find out all we can about his disappearance."

Ben scowled at his sister. "I haven't forgotten," he said. "I've got the recording of Mat's voice ready to play as soon as we're alone."

"Ready?" interrupted an eager voice.

Mat was back. He handed them each a pair of binoculars and a paper bag. "There are rusks for the orangutans in here," he said. "They love them."

He led them along a narrow pathway through the trees. Harsh warning cries rang out in response to the sound of their footsteps.

"Proboscis monkeys," said Mat. "Very nervous animals."

Mat stopped at a huge climbing frame of reddish wood. A ladder led up to a high platform that stretched from tree to tree.

Ben grabbed the rungs of the ladder, preparing to climb. "I can't wait!" he said.

"Great to see you're so eager, Ben," said Mat. "I suppose this is the first time you'll come face to face with real wild animals, yes?"

Ben and Zoe smiled.

"If any animal comes close, just stay calm," Mat said. "We're sure to come across some orangutans. They're peaceful animals — and very curious. They'll probably come to inspect you. The walkways are safe and every platform has an escape ladder. But enough safety talk. Let's climb!"

Soon, they reached the top of the ladder and stepped onto the platform. A walkway made of wood was connected to long ropes. It stretched far into the distance.

Zoe decided it was a good time to start gathering information. "I wish we could see . . . what was the name of the young orangutan that's missing?" she asked innocently.

"Kawan," said Mat. "We'll go to the area that used to be his territory. I keep hoping he'll show up there."

Mat stepped onto the walkway, grasping the handrails. It swayed gently under his weight. The children followed him eagerly along the path from tree to tree.

Frogs croaked, macaques screeched as they swung from tree to tree, and parrots cawed from nearby branches.

At each platform, there were
informational posters about the creatures to
watch for. Ben studied each one.

"What are those?" asked Zoe, pointing
at some odd-looking birds perched above
their heads. "It looks they have horns on
their beaks."

"Didn't you read the sign?" Ben said,
teasing Zoe. "They're called rhinoceros
birds."

There was a loud rustling of leaves and suddenly two orangutans burst into view, swinging after each other across the interwoven branches.

"That's Lola and Kiki," Mat told them. "They're mother and daughter. They'll probably come say hello in a minute or two."

The two apes suddenly stopped playing when they spotted the humans. With a terrified shriek, they turned and disappeared among the dense trees.

Zoe looked disappointed. "Did we scare them away?" she asked.

"I don't think so," Mat said, frowning. "But I'm surprised they left so quickly. They're usually very friendly."

Mat stopped and looked around. "Come to think of it," he said, "it's been quieter than usual today. We've been through several territories and we've only seen Lola and Kiki."

Mat shrugged. He led them around a platform, down a ladder, and onto a lower walkway. "We're just coming into Kawan's old patch now," he said.

Ben gave Zoe a thumbs up. Maybe they'd learn something useful here.

The walkway took them alongside a wide, muddy river. "This is the Munia River," Mat told them.

Zoe recognized some straight rows of low-growing trees. They looked very different from the natural tangle of the high rainforest. "Those are oil palms growing on the other side, aren't they?" she asked.

"That's Mr. Ostriander's land," Mat said. "We're in the southeastern corner of the reservation now."

Mat led them onto a wide platform that hung from a tree with a thick trunk. A metal sign that read "PLATFORM 22" hung above a map of the walkways.

The river wound its way into the distance, separating the palm trees from a wide piece of flat land. Small plants in metal drums were growing at regular intervals.

"New oil palms," Mat said, pointing at the metal drums. "That's where Daud spotted Kawan. I've tried calling him from here, but I don't think the sound travels that far."

"I hope he comes back soon," said Zoe.

"I'd love you to meet Kawan," said Mat. "He's such a character, and a great imitator. He used to fill up pans with rice and beans and stir them with a spoon, just like Yasmin does when she cooks." Mat looked over the edge of the walkway. "It might not work, but I'll try calling him again."

Mat pursed his lips together and made the call Zoe and Ben had heard earlier in the video.

Ben and Zoe walked around to the opposite side of the platform. They could see an area filled with tree stumps. It looked like an ugly wound in the middle of the dense rainforest.

Zoe looked at the devastation. "Those evil loggers," she said. "I'm glad they were chased off before they did more damage. Poor Kawan must have been so frightened by them."

"I wish I could play my recording," Ben whispered to Zoe. "At full volume, Kawan would be sure to hear it if he's anywhere nearby."

Mat stopped calling for Kawan and came to join them.

"No luck, I'm afraid," Mat said. He pointed to the damaged area. "Kawan always nested near there."

"Nested?" Zoe asked. "Like bird nests?"

Mat grinned. He pointed up at the treeline. "Orangutans make themselves a different bed every night up in the tree canopy," he said. "They even use big leaves as blankets."

Zoe nodded. "Oh, yeah," she said. "I think I've read about that."

"Sometimes they use them as umbrellas or sunshades," Mat went on. He was about to say more when a shrill beeping from his shirt pocket distracted him. "Sorry about this," he said, pulling out a walkie-talkie. "It must be Yasmin back at the center."

He turned away and spoke rapidly in Malay.

Ben and Zoe heard Yasmin's voice translated through their earpieces. "Something's wrong," her voice said. "We have another cancellation. This time it's the Coopers."

"They were coming next week, weren't they?" asked Mat.

His walkie-talkie buzzed and Yasmin spoke again. "They thought they were still coming this week, despite the closing," she said. "Good thing they emailed to ask about it. How could this happen?"

"I'm not sure," Mat said into the walkie-talkie. "But I'll come back right now. We'll phone everyone and reinstate their bookings. Then we'll look into it. It probably has something to do with our old fossil of a computer."

He turned to Ben and Zoe.

"Sorry," Mat said. "We have to return now, but I promise we'll come again tomorrow morning." He turned and headed along the walkway back toward the reservation.

Ben stopped Zoe from following after him. "We haven't had a chance to play the recording yet," Ben whispered.

"Then we come back tonight," said Zoe. "By ourselves."

CHAPTER 5

SECRET MISSION

Zoe crept across the bare wooden floor of their bedroom and nudged Ben through his mosquito net. "Wake up," she whispered. "We've got two hours until sunrise."

Ben opened his eyes and sat up in the dark. "Let's go," he said.

They dressed quickly and put on their backpacks. They'd filled them the night before with water, a first aid kit, and their BUGs.

Then they put on their EEL belts and boots, and snatched up their night goggles.

Zoe slowly opened the door. "Shh!" Ben whispered as the hinges squeaked.

They stepped outside into the silent, shadowy compound. As soon as they put on their goggles, the scene was bathed in green light. They could even see water dripping from the trees into puddles below.

"Looks like we just missed a shower," Ben whispered.

Zoe nodded. She turned a dial on goggles' nosepiece to adjust the focus. "We'll follow the satellite map on the BUGs," she said.

They crept toward the cover of the trees. "The black zigzag lines are the walkways," Zoe said as she studied the map on her BUG screen.

"They lead to Kawan's territory where the walkways meet the river," Ben said.

"Is there a more direct path?" asked Zoe.

Ben pressed a button on his BUG and a different map appeared.

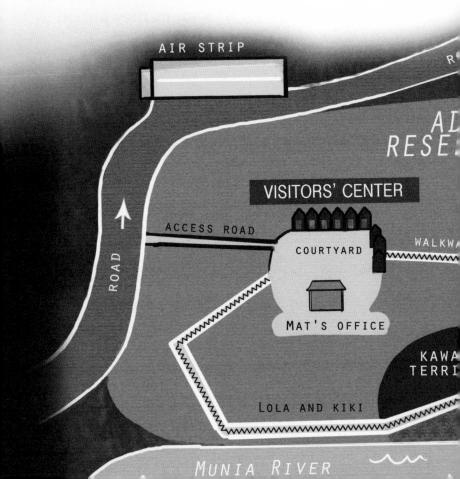

This map showed a narrow trail that led right to the southeast edge of the reservation. "This will get us there faster," Ben said.

"Tuck your pants into your boots," Zoe said. "There will be snakes."

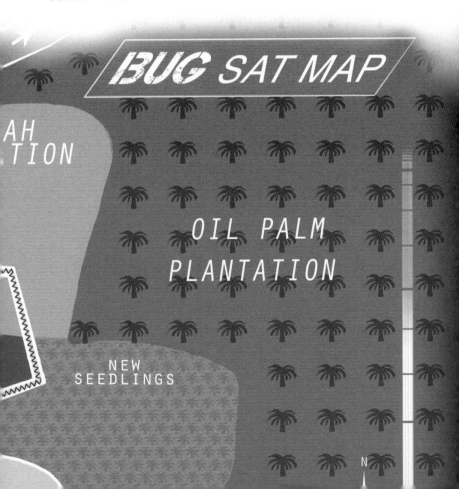

BUG SAT MAP

AH
TION

OIL PALM
PLANTATION

NEW
SEEDLINGS

N

"And other creepy-crawlies," Ben said.

"Scent dispersers on, too," Zoe said. "That will help keep us safe from predators."

The rough path led deep into the darkness of the rainforest. The children moved along as quietly as they could, listening carefully to the sounds around them.

Suddenly there was a loud animal call. A long, skinny shape swung down in front of them. It peered at them from under a pair of thick eyebrows. The children stopped dead, hearts beating fast. Then the creature let out a cry and hurried back up into the trees.

Zoe checked her BUG's analysis of the creature. "It was a gibbon!" she whispered. "Wonder what it thought of our goggled faces!"

"Look at that!" Ben said, pointing into the darkness. "Around that tree trunk. It looks like a huge snake!"

"You spaz," Zoe said, laughing. "It's just a root that's twisted around the tree."

Ben let out a sigh of relief. "Oh, shut up," he said. "I just don't like snakes."

They pushed their way through a bank of thick fern leaves that hung across the path.

"I can hear the river," Ben said. "We must be in Kawan's territory now. The walkways should be right above us."

"There's a sign on that trunk," said Zoe, pointing. "Platform 22 — that's where we were earlier. We're here."

Something moved along the ground ahead of them.

Through their goggles, Ben and Zoe caught a glimpse of cold reptilian eyes and a scaly snout. "Crocodile!" Ben said, pulling Zoe back. "We have to get off the ground — now!"

"But how?" Zoe said. She looked around in a panic.

"There's a ladder up to the platform," Ben said. He stumbled through the ferns to reach the numbered trunk. Zoe followed.

Behind Zoe, the ferns swayed and flattened as the crocodile gave chase.

Ben leaped up the first rungs of the wooden ladder. He reached down and grabbed Zoe's hand, hauling her up to safety just as the crocodile launched itself at the base of the tree and snapped its jaws at the empty air beneath her feet.

"That was close!" Zoe said, scrambling up as high as she could. "I thought we were safe with our scent dispersers on."

"Crocodiles have great hearing," Ben said. He looked down at the enormous scaly creature beneath them. "We weren't exactly silent back there, either."

Ben could tell Zoe was a little spooked. "Did you know," he said as they climbed toward the platform, "that crocodiles can grow up to twenty-two feet long?"

"Yikes," said Zoe. "Then there's plenty of room inside their stomachs for a couple of kids like us!" Ben laughed.

Soon, they arrived on the platform. Down below, they could see the shape of their attacker sliding back toward the dark sweep of the river just beyond the trees.

"This is a good place to try the call," Ben said. He pulled out his BUG and pressed a few buttons. A loud chirping noise filled the air. It echoed far into the trees.

"It would have been better to do this in the day," said Zoe. "Then Kawan would be awake."

"We have no choice," Ben said, smiling. "Besides, I'm sure he'll forgive us for waking him up."

They sat as still as they could, carefully scanning the area through their goggles. "Fruit bats, several otters, and two monkeys," reported Zoe. "But no orangutans."

Ben played the call again and again. "Looks like Kawan's not here," he said at last. "Maybe we should be heading back —"

Ben stopped. There was a rustling in the branches above their heads, followed by a loud chomping sound. Zoe quickly held out her BUG towards it to analyze the sound. "It's an orangutan!" she whispered.

Ben narrowed his eyes and ducked down. "The BUG says that sound means it feels threatened," he said.

"Stay still, then," said Zoe. "It has to be Kawan — he's responded to the call."

Ben clicked the ZOOM button his goggles. Zoe did the same. "Wow," whispered Zoe, pointing upward. "He's right above our heads."

A dark shape was soaring through the high branches. Ben wriggled around and held his BUG above the leaves, activating its camera function. "Got a photo," he whispered.

They peered down at the screen. The face of a familiar young orangutan stared back at them. He had a distinctive tuft of hair sticking up on one side of his head, just like they'd seen in the film.

"Awesome!" said Ben. "It's Kawan!"

CHAPTER 6

KAWAN

The young orangutan sat in the branches above their heads. He gazed at Ben and Zoe, his eyes flickering nervously.

"I have a biscuit in my backpack," Zoe said quietly. "Let's see if we can tempt him down and make him feel safe."

"Mat's going to be so happy," said Ben.

Moving in slow motion, Zoe stood and held the biscuit above her head.

Kawan began to swing gracefully down from branch to branch. When he stopped, he was just out of reach, hanging from one long, shaggy arm. He looked tense and ready to escape at the slightest threat.

"Do you think he's wondering where Mat is?" asked Ben. "I hope he doesn't leave when he realizes that Mat's not here."

"Come on, Kawan," Zoe said gently. "Here, boy." She waved the biscuit.

Kawan hesitated. Then he extended one leathery hand and took the biscuit. Eyes firmly fixed on them, he solemnly nibbled at the treat, dropping the crumbs around their feet.

"He still looks very nervous," said Ben. "Those loggers must have really scared him."

"He wouldn't come so close if he didn't trust us," said Zoe, pulling out another rusk to hand to the young ape. "Something must be telling him we're not a threat. Maybe it was Mat's call."

Kawan held out a crumb-covered finger and touched Zoe's cheek. She sighed with delight. "I can see why Mat's so fond of him," she said. "He's adorable."

Kawan dropped down on to the platform and reached out for the second rusk.

"Good boy, Kawan," Ben whispered.

At that moment, the sound of an explosion filled the air. Without thinking, the children threw themselves down onto the wooden slats.

With a terrified shriek, Kawan leaped into the trees, swinging away into the darkness. Soon he was out of sight.

"Was that a gunshot?" Zoe asked, horrified.

"I don't think so," said Ben, gripping Zoe's arm. "But I've heard that sort of sound before somewhere. Someone's down there, heading through the undergrowth."

They looked down over the side of the slats. A shadowy figure was hurrying along the ground.

"It's a man," whispered Ben. "What's he doing here at this time of night?"

"Let's follow him," Zoe said.

Moving swiftly along the swaying walkway, they followed the sound until they reached the next platform. "This is where we saw Lola and Kiki," whispered Zoe. "The walkway after this is much higher. There's a ladder somewhere here."

Zoe found the top of the ladder and climbed up to the next platform, feeling for each rung in the dark.

"Hurry," Ben said. "He's getting away."

Zoe didn't need to be told twice. She raced ahead of her brother along the wobbly wooden slats of the walkway.

CRACK! There was a loud splitting sound under her feet. She heard Ben's cry of alarm as she felt herself falling.

CHAPTER 7

LOUD NOISES

Zoe flung out her arms and grabbed desperately at the broken walkway. Her hands closed around a wooden slat. She felt her arms being almost jerked out of their sockets as she came to a sudden stop. She held on with all her strength, not daring to look at the ground.

"Hold on," Ben called, trying to keep the panic out of his voice. She could just see Ben crouched on the walkway, one hand reaching out to pull her to safety.

Then something else caught her eye. The ropes that supported the slatted walkway were worn down to a single strand!

"Get back, Ben!" she shouted. "The whole thing's about to fall!"

There was a ripping sound as the last strand of rope split. Zoe felt herself jolting downward, falling away from the platform.

Ben had a split second to react. He slammed the button on his belt and felt a cord shoot out from his boots toward the trees. He dived off the platform. As he fell, he grabbed onto Zoe by the straps of her backpack. Together they tumbled through the air.

For a second, a whirl of dark undergrowth flashed in front of their eyes. The ground came toward them dizzyingly fast.

Then, suddenly, they were jerked upward again. "Good ol' Uncle Stephen!" Ben yelled. "That certainly tested out his EEL device."

They finally came to a stop, dangling above the ground and twisting slowly.

Ben checked the terrain below. "Not a crocodile in sight," he said. "Prepare for landing." He put his thumb over one of the buttons on the gadget at his waist and gradually lowered them both to the ground.

"For once, you were listening when Erika told us about our new gadget!" said Zoe, dropping safely to the ground. "I'm glad I had my backpack strapped on securely."

Ben flipped the far end of the EEL line off its branch and retracted it. Then he looked up at the broken walkway dangling high above their heads.

"We've lost our prey," said Ben. "He's probably far away now."

"But at least we know what he was up to," Zoe said.

Ben had a puzzled look on his face.

"There's no way that was an accident," Zoe explained grimly. "When the wood cracked, I could see it had been sawed most of the way through — just enough to break under the weight of a person."

Ben gasped. "He must have cut through the ropes, too," he said.

"Those walkways were fine when we were here this afternoon," said Zoe. "And I bet he had something to do with those banging sounds, as well. Whatever they were."

"Our mission's not going to be as straightforward as we thought." Ben said.

"You're right," said Zoe. "Someone's targeting the reservation."

Zoe had a sudden thought. "Maybe the booking cancellations weren't just a mistake," she said. "Do you think those loggers who scared off Kawan are behind it all?"

"Whoever it is," Ben said, "I bet it's someone who knows Mat."

"How can you be sure?" asked Zoe.

"Mat said he takes the same route every day to call Kawan," Ben said. "Only Mat's friends and people who work with him would know that. He would have stepped on the sabotaged walkway and fallen — and he wouldn't have had an EEL to save him."

"Do you think Mat realizes someone's out to get him?" asked Zoe.

"If he does, he's not going to tell us," said Ben. "He thinks we're just visitors."

Zoe nodded. "We have to talk to Mat about the walkway right away," she said.

"How's that going to look?" said Ben. "We can't just tell him we were out looking for Kawan at four a.m."

"You're right," agreed Ben. "He'll see it in the morning, anyway."

Zoe bent down and picked up a silver strip of paper from the ground. She held it out toward Ben.

"It looks like a chewing gum wrapper," Ben said with a shrug.

"It could be a clue," replied Zoe. "Whoever sabotaged the walkway must have dropped it just now."

"How did you figure that out, detective?" Ben said, teasing his sister. "It could have been here for days!"

"That's where you're wrong." Zoe grinned. "This wrapper's perfectly dry. It rained before we came out, so it must have been dropped after that. And who else would be out here in the middle of the night?"

"Good thinking!" said Ben. "You're smarter than you look."

Zoe rolled her eyes and slipped the chewing gum wrapper into her pocket. Then she rubbed her shoulders under the backpack straps and stretched. "I thought you were going to pull my arms out of their sockets when we fell," she said.

"Sorry," said Ben. He grinned. "I'll remember not to save your life next time!"

Zoe took her BUG and pressed some buttons to bring up the satellite map of the area. "Let's get back before the sun rises," she said.

They hurried away, pushing through the undergrowth. They hadn't gone far when Zoe suddenly went sprawling.

"Ow!" she groaned, rubbing her shin.

She looked around. "There's some sort of rock or something in those ferns," Zoe said.

When they looked closer, they saw that it was a metallic object. Ben held his BUG over the strange device. "The BUG says it's a bird scarer," he said. "They make loud noises to scare away birds."

"We saw how terrified Kawan was just now," Zoe said, "and no wonder Lola and Kiki were looking so nervous earlier."

"Someone is deliberately trying to frighten the orangutans," Ben said. "Kawan might have come back before but been scared away each time."

Zoe gritted her teeth. "I'm going to put a stop to it," she said, giving the box a hard kick. "Ow!"

"That won't do it," said Ben. He put his fingers under the edge of the metal cover and pried it open. Inside was a battery and a timer. It was set to go off early each morning. He wrenched the wires off the battery and put the cover back in place. He grinned at his sister. "Now nobody but us knows that it doesn't work."

* * *

The birds' morning chorus filled their ears as the children crept back through the courtyard. The air had become hot and still.

The minute they closed their door, a sudden flash of lightning lit the bedroom. Thunder crashed overhead as a torrent of rain began hammering down like a waterfall outside their window.

"Glad we didn't get caught in that!" said Ben.

"I hope that evil man did," said Zoe, pacing back and forth. "We have to find out who he is."

Ben let out a big yawn. "Not now," he said, lifting the mosquito net. He flopped onto his bed. "We have to wait for Mat to discover the broken boards. Let's get some sleep."

Ben dozed off almost immediately. Zoe, however, lay awake for a long time. She kept imagining how terrified poor Kawan must be right now. After a while, she fell into a restless sleep.

CHAPTER 8

BREAKFAST

"Daud, Talib!" A distant voice speaking in Malay broke through Zoe's dreams. She groggily slipped her translator into her ear. "Come quickly," she heard, "and bring your tools!"

Zoe shook Ben awake, then pulled on some long pants and a T-shirt. She put her BUG into her pocket and crept out. Ben followed behind her, blinking sleepily in the daylight. They watched from the shadows of the doorway that opened to the compound.

Yasmin was standing barefoot among the steaming puddles. She looked nervous as she watched her husband run up to her. Biza clung to her shoulders.

"It's okay," Mat said. He put his hand on her shoulder. "One of the walkways broke."

"He's found it already!" Ben whispered to his sister. "Maybe now he'll realize there's something strange going on."

"It was probably the storm earlier," Mat went on. "I am so thankful it didn't happen when anyone was on the walkway."

"Are you sure it was just the storm?" said Yasmin. "We've had such bad luck lately. Do you think it could be the loggers from before?"

"They wouldn't dare," said Mat calmly. "Try not to worry."

Just then, Daud appeared with the tools. Mat spotted Ben and Zoe standing in the doorway and walked over to them. "I'm sorry, Ben and Zoe," he said with a regretful smile. "I have to make some emergency repairs to one of the walkways this morning. But I'll be back this afternoon with a surprise for you. In the meantime, Yasmin will look after you."

He turned to Daud and told him what had happened in Malay. "Where's Talib?" Ben and Zoe heard him ask.

"He was chopping wood just now," said Daud. "I don't think he heard you call."

As he spoke, Talib came around the corner behind him. He was carrying a pile of logs. A strange expression flashed across his face when he saw Mat standing in front of him.

"That's odd," muttered Zoe, as the two workers followed Mat into the forest. "Did you see how Talib reacted?"

"He's probably annoyed that he's got some extra work to do," said Ben.

Mat's wife turned toward the door where Ben and Zoe were. "Is everything all right?" Ben asked holding the door open for her to go through. "You look worried."

"Just a broken walkway," said Yasmin. She gave a weak smile. Ben and Zoe realized Yasmin didn't share her husband's optimistic perspective of the recent events.

"Would you like some breakfast?" Yasmin asked. She showed them into the kitchen. "We have *nasi lemak*, which is rice boiled in coconut milk."

"Sounds delicious," Ben said.

Yasmin smiled. "It is quite delicious," she said. Her smile faded. "But I must ask for a favor — could one of you hold Biza for me while I make breakfast? He is a naughty boy. He always tries to steal my food."

"That's Zoe's territory," Ben said, chuckling. Yasmin unwrapped the baby orangutan's arms and held him out.

Zoe grinned and took Biza. The little ape looked doubtful for a moment, but climbed slowly onto her shoulder. Zoe could feel his breath on her neck — and then his hand pulling her BUG out of her pocket! Zoe gave a cry and quickly grabbed hold of it before Biza could put it in his mouth.

As she tussled with his surprisingly strong hands, she heard the sound of deep laughter from the doorway. Mr. Ostriander came in.

"You'll never get Biza to behave," he said. "He runs the show here. Isn't that right, Yasmin?"

Yasmin looked up from the cooker. "Morning, Peter," she said with a smile. "And yes, he may be the smallest of our apes, but he's definitely in charge." She waved him to a seat. "You remember Ben and Zoe, right?"

"Good to see you again," said Mr. Ostriander. He turned to Zoe, who was still struggling to put her BUG back in her pocket. "Be careful, or that little fellow will make off with your portable video game."

Zoe grinned. Thankfully, Mr. Ostriander didn't look very closely at the BUG or he would've known it was far more than a gaming device.

"I'm afraid you've missed Mat," Yasmin told Mr. Ostriander. "He left to make some repairs to one of the walkways."

"Storm damage?" Mr. Ostriander asked. "We had some violent weather last night."

"Probably," said Yasmin. She put the *nasi lemak* on plates for the children.

Biza finally gave up the struggle for Zoe's BUG. He dropped to the floor and went straight for Mr. Ostriander's boot lace.

Yasmin scooped Biza up. "Come on, you little troublemaker," she said. "It's time for your nap."

"What have you two got planned today?" asked Mr. Ostriander.

"We're not sure yet," Ben said. "But Mat planned a surprise for us later this afternoon."

"How big is your plantation, Mr. Ostriander?" Zoe asked suddenly. "Do you know how many trees you have?"

"That's a difficult one," Peter Ostriander replied, smiling. "There are so many, you see."

"And what kind of tractors do you use?" Zoe asked. "I bet they're awesome!"

Ben stared at Zoe wondering, why his sister was suddenly interested in the details of oil palm farming.

"Tell you what," said Mr. Ostriander, "since you're so interested, why don't you come and take a look for yourselves?"

Ben saw Zoe grinning at him. *So that's what her plan is!* he thought. She'd gotten them an invitation to the plantation. Zoe was hoping they'd get a glimpse of Kawan or find some clues about last night's events.

CHAPTER 9

PLANTATION PLOT

Zoe and Ben stood at the prow of Mr. Ostriander's speedboat. They watched it cut through the water of the Munia River.

Peter had already showed them the processing plant. He had given them tons of food in a very posh dining room afterward. Now they were off to see the plantation fields of oil palms up close.

On the right bank of the river were the rows of oil palm trees Mat had pointed out from the walkway.

The rainforest trees of the reservation spread to the left. They could hear the sound of distant hammering coming from somewhere among them.

"That must be Mat and his men seeing to the repairs," Zoe whispered to Ben. "They'll have to go and check the whole thing after that. It'll take ages."

"Here's that bend in the river we saw yesterday," whispered Ben. "We must be coming to Kawan's old territory."

"That means beyond it is the reservation boundary," Zoe said, "and the new palm oil plants."

"Yep, that's near where Mat said Kawan was spotted," said Ben. "We have to get a look among those trees somehow. But of course, we can't just ask."

"Why not?" said Zoe. "We don't have to say anything about WILD."

Holding on to the safety rail, Zoe made her way back to the cabin where Mr. Ostriander was at the wheel. "Has Mat told you about the missing orangutan?" Zoe asked.

A serious look spread across Mr. Ostriander's face. "Ah yes, Kawan," he said. "Mat was very upset about his disappearance."

Mr. Ostriander shrugged. "I've heard the little fella has been spotted among my trees," he said, "although I haven't seen him myself."

Zoe pointed ahead to where the land had been cleared. "Could we go look for him?" she asked. Then she added quickly, "I'd just love to be able to say I've seen him so we can tell Mat that he's still all right."

"Of course," said Mr. Ostriander. He steered the speedboat to a small landing on the left bank. He cut the engine.

"As you can see, these are my newest trees," Mr. Ostriander told them as they walked between the oil drums. "They'll be producing fruit for oil production in about four years. I've increased my workforce by ten percent for these trees, so it's been good for the local economy."

Ben looked at Zoe. He could guess what she was thinking. They had to pretend they were interested until they got to the mature trees.

Mr. Ostriander pointed over to a new red roofed shed in the distance. "That's where the next crop of oil palm fruit will be stored," he said. "Then it will be taken to the processing factory."

Just then, Mr. Ostriander's cell phone rang. "I have to take this call," he said. "Please have a look around. Let me know if you see Kawan." He flipped open his phone and walked away.

Zoe and Ben didn't waste any time. They ran between the rows of seedlings until they reached the lines of trees. Keeping the edge of the seedling patch in sight, they walked among the low branches of the oil palms.

They heard the calls of unseen creatures. Ben held up his BUG and pressed a button. "I'm analyzing the calls," he said. "No orangutans. They're just birds."

Zoe pointed into the distance. "Isn't that Talib?" she said. "There, coming out of the little door at the end of the shed."

Ben got his binoculars out and zoomed in. He saw a figure carrying a heavy can.

"It's Talib," Ben said, surprised. "What's he doing on Mr. Ostriander's land? He's supposed to be helping Mat repair the walkways."

They crept toward the tall, wooden shed. Then they peered around to watch Talib. He stopped, put down the can, and pulled out something from his pocket.

He unwrapped it, placed it in his mouth, and began to chew. He threw the wrapper to the ground, then picked up the can and walked off into the trees.

"Did you see that?" said Zoe. When Talib was out of sight, she ran over and picked up the silver wrapper. "This is just like the one I found last night. Do you think it was Talib who sabotaged the walkway?"

"Let's take a look inside the shed," Ben said.

They slipped inside. Rakes, spades, and machetes lined the walls. A dirty old tarp had been thrown in one corner. Ben pulled it back to reveal four more cans just like the one Talib had taken. Ben picked it up and shook it. He heard liquid inside.

Zoe sniffed. "It's gasoline!" she said. "But why would Talib be stealing gas?"

"If you're right about the gum," said Ben, "then it was Talib who sabotaged the walkway and put the bird scarer in place." Ben's face grew grim. "And I'd be willing to bet that he's planning to set the reservation on fire next!"

CHAPTER 10

SURPRISE

Mr. Ostriander chatted with Ben and
Zoe as he drove them back to the Adilah
Reservation. They sat in the back, trying to
act as if nothing was wrong.

Ben remembered the strange expression
on Talib's face when Mat told him about
the broken walkway. He must have been
surprised that Mat was still in one piece. Ben
needed to find out more about Talib. Maybe
Mr. Ostriander could help, but how could
Ben bring it up without seeming suspicious?

"Too bad there was no sign of Kawan," Mr. Ostriander said.

"I'm sure Mat will keep looking," said Ben. "And his staff," he added with a sudden flash of inspiration. "We know that Daud really likes him."

"But we don't know anything about Talib," Zoe said, catching on to Ben's plan. "He's very quiet. Do you know what he's like, Mr. Ostriander?"

"I don't know Mat's workers very well," said the plantation owner. "Which one is Talib?"

"The older one with gray hair," Ben told him.

"The cranky fella?" Mr. Ostriander said, shrugging. "Never spoken to him." He swung the jeep through the gates of the reservation.

Mat was waiting for them in the courtyard. They climbed out of the car and headed toward Mat.

"You're back just in time for your surprise treat," Mat announced. "I'll let you go and clean yourselves up first. Meet you back here in five minutes."

Back in their room, Ben said, "Our surprise came at the worst time."

Zoe nodded. "What are we going to do about Talib?" she asked. "He could start the fire at any moment. We have to tell Mat."

"We can't," said Ben. "We'd have to tell him about the walkway and the shed. He can't know that we've been investigating."

"Then we'll call Uncle Stephen," Zoe said. She pulled out her BUG and pressed the hot key that dialed WILD HQ.

"Greetings!" they heard their uncle's sleepy voice say. It was the middle of the night on his island. "Any news about Kawan yet?"

"We've seen him," said Zoe. "But there's much more to tell."

After Zoe finished her report, Uncle Stephen was silent for a moment. "Worse than I thought," he finally said. "Erika's in North Borneo — I'll ask her to anonymously alert the authorities right now. They take fire in the forest very seriously. I'm sure they'll be on their way at once."

"And as soon as the threat's over, we'll try using the call again to lure Kawan back to his old territory," added Zoe. "There's no bird scarer to keep him away now."

"You go and enjoy your surprise," said their uncle. "Leave the rest to me."

"Are you ready?" they heard Mat calling from the courtyard. They swung on their backpacks and headed outside to find him standing by a small jeep. He grinned when he saw them. "Hop in!"

Mat steered the jeep down a bumpy trail. It was impossible to see ahead because of the dense trees. "Where are we going?" asked Zoe.

"You'll see in a minute," Mat said coyly.

The jeep turned a corner and entered a cleared area about the size of a football field. It led to a runway. Ben and Zoe could see that it was a small airstrip. Then they spotted a strange craft shimmering in the heat in the middle of the tarmac.

"A hot-air balloon!" Ben said.

Zoe gave a cheer of delight. "Are we going for a ride?" she asked.

"Yep!" Mat said, beaming. "It's the best way to see the rainforest."

They hurried toward the balloon, which was still being filled with hot air.

"Maybe our surprise came at a good time after all," Zoe whispered to Ben.

Ben frowned. "Why do you say that?" he asked.

"If a fire does start, now we can see exactly where it is and put out an alert immediately," Zoe said.

* * *

WHOOSH! Mat turned up the flame under the huge red balloon. A man untied the ropes. Ben and Zoe felt the basket rise up into the air. "And we're off!" Mat said.

"It's so bumpy!" Zoe yelled over the noise of the roaring flame.

Mat smiled. "You get used to it," he said.

They were soon at the height of the treetops. Mat pulled on a cord. "This opens the parachute valve a little," he told them.

Mat saw the concern on their faces. "Don't worry, we're not jumping!" he said. "It just lets out hot air to stop us from traveling any higher. Can you feel the tug on the basket? At different heights, the winds travel in different directions. We've reached a patch of wind that's blowing southeast, which is just what we need to pass over the reservation."

"If we have to change direction, do we just go up or down to catch a different wind?" Ben asked.

"You've got it!" said Mat. "I can't guarantee we'll land in the middle of the tarmac, but I've yet to miss an airstrip while landing."

Above the forest canopy, the air felt fresher. Ben and Zoe could feel a welcome breeze on their skin.

Mat proudly gestured over his land. "This is all the Adilah Reservation," he said.

The tops of the tallest trees reached out but didn't quite touch each other. Small trees filled the gaps below. It looked like an endless sea of green. "Some of the trees are 225 feet tall," explained Mat. "All sorts of creatures live up there, including monkeys, spiders, snakes, and lizards."

Zoe screened her eyes as she looked at a barren peak far in the distance. "What's that mountain over there?" she asked.

"Mount Kinabalu," said Mat. He handed them binoculars. "You'll have a good view of it now that we're so high."

"I don't like the look of the dark clouds over it," said Ben. "Are we going to get rained on?"

"They're far away," Mat said. "We should be back before it rains. I'm going to take you right across the reservation. We're at the southeastern point here. You can see the oil palms stretching all the way to the edge of my land."

"There are the seedlings," said Zoe. "It looks like a connect-the-dots puzzle from here."

"This will bring the tourists in," said Ben. "You'll be so busy that you'll need to recruit more staff."

"Maybe," said Mat, laughing. "I'll manage with Daud and Talib for the moment."

Zoe caught Ben's eye. "Have they worked with you for long?" she asked.

"Daud and I went to school together," Mat told her. "Talib works for Mr. Ostriander. Peter is just lending him to me for a short while. He said I'd need more help with the reservation opening." He stepped to the other side of the basket to check the balloon's position with his map.

"I don't understand," Ben whispered in Zoe's ear. "Mr. Ostriander said he didn't know Talib."

Despite the heat Zoe felt a chill run up her back. "Why would he lie?" she whispered back. "He's a friend of Mat's."

Ben suddenly grasped Zoe by the shoulders. "That's what he wanted us to think. But don't you remember? Mat said Mr. Ostriander wanted to buy Adilah when he first bought his plantation. It all makes sense now! When Mat wouldn't sell, Mr. Ostriander decided to get it another way."

"So you think Ostriander's the one behind the cancellations, the broken walkway, and scaring away the orangutans — and Kawan, too?" Zoe asked.

Ben nodded. "All that stuff about helping Mat was probably just a cover," he said. "He sent Talib to work for him and secretly carry out his evil plans."

"How smart," Zoe said. "Ostriander appeared to be a hero when he had the loggers chased off. But I bet he sent them there in the first place!"

Ben nodded. "He's been trying to make sure that the reservation fails," he said. "I guess he's planning to step in as soon as it does and then buy the land so he can expand his plantation."

At that moment, the flame above them puttered and flickered. Mat turned the ring on one of the propane cylinders and frowned. "It's out of gas already?" he said. "That's strange. I'm sure the other two gas cylinders are okay, though." He quickly opened the valve on another cylinder, but there was no burst of fire from overhead. Ben and Zoe could see that Mat looked worried.

"I don't understand it," Mat muttered. "I told Talib to fill them for the trip."

Ben and Zoe shared a horrified expression. "Talib filled the cylinders?!" Zoe whispered to Ben.

Ben quickly kneeled down by one of them. A tiny blob of chewing gum had been squeezed in under the needle. "Look inside the glass!" Ben shouted. "Talib used his chewing gum to wedge the gauge so it looks full."

Mat twisted the third valve open, but no gas came out. "They've been tampered with!" he cried. "Why would Talib do this?!"

Over their heads, the flame spluttered, then died. Ben and Zoe felt the wind throb in their ears as the balloon began to drop. The sides of the nylon envelope, no longer filled with heat, flapped loudly in the downward rush toward the dense green of the forest below.

"Get down as low as you can!" shouted Mat. "Brace yourselves for the impact. With luck, we'll hit the canopy and our fall will be softened."

Ben and Zoe could see how close they were to the open land of the oil palm plantation. If they crash-landed there, they didn't stand a chance.

CHAPTER 11

CRASH LANDING

Zoe shrieked as she felt the basket smash down on top of the trees, throwing her against Ben. The deafening crack of breaking branches filled the air.

The basket tumbled down through the canopy, almost flinging Ben over the side. Zoe grasped his arm and pulled him back in. They held on to each other, huddled in one corner of the basket. Suddenly the basket gave a huge jolt and came to rest at a crooked angle.

The basket swung from side to side, the balloon envelope tangled in the branches above. "We've stopped falling!" said Zoe, pulling herself up by one of the ropes.

Ben peered over the basket's edge. "The balloon's caught on a tree," he said. "We're safe — for now."

"But look at Mat!" Zoe said. She edged her way slowly over to where their pilot lay in a crumpled heap.

"Is he alive?" Ben asked. As he moved to get closer, the basket rocked dangerously.

Zoe felt Mat's pulse. "His pulse is fine," she said. "He must have been knocked out when we fell."

Ben pulled out his BUG. "I'm going to call Uncle Stephen," he said. "He can get help —"

Suddenly, some of the balloon fabric ripped. The basket fell to the branch below.

"There's no time," Zoe said urgently. "We've got to get down to the ground right now."

"We can use our EELs," said Ben. "I'll take Mat."

Zoe pressed the button on her EEL belt. As she leaped out of the basket, she felt the cord fasten to the branches above.

Ben gripped Mat tightly around the waist and prepared to jump. He knew he had to get them out of the basket, which was starting to rock dangerously. Mat was like a dead weight in his arms. Ben couldn't move him at all.

There was a crack of snapping wood and the basket broke loose from the tree.

Ben fired his EEL as he felt himself being thrown into the air. He clung to Mat as hard as he could while they plummeted. Ben hoped they weren't too heavy for the EEL's wire. Then, to his relief, he felt the jerk of the cord.

As soon as Mat was safely down on the ground, Zoe felt his pulse. "It's very weak," she said, worried. "And he looks so pale."

"We need to get him medical help as soon as possible," said Ben. "I'll call Uncle Stephen now."

The chugging sound of a four-wheeler burst through the trees. "Someone must have seen the balloon come down," Ben said. "Help's arrived!"

"And they've got transportation," said Zoe excitedly. "They can take Mat to the hospital!"

She jumped to her feet and waved her arms. "We're over here!" she cried.

But then their hope turned to dread. Their rescuer was no rescuer at all. It was Peter Ostriander. He shut off the engine, dismounted, and ran over to them.

Out of the corner of her eye, Zoe saw Ben's fingers reaching for his BUG. She ran forward to Mr. Ostriander to block his view.

"Thank goodness you're here," Zoe cried. "There's been an accident. Mat's hurt."

"I saw the balloon come down," Mr. Ostriander said in a concerned tone. "What a dreadful accident." He walked over to Mat.

"No accident," Mat groaned. His eyes flickered open. "Talib did this. You did this."

"Oh, dear," said Mr. Ostriander. His voice was suddenly harsh as he gazed down at Mat. "If you hadn't figured that out, I might have rescued you and continued this little charade. But now I can't let you live to tell your tale, or it'll ruin my grand plans."

A look of utter disbelief spread over Mat's face. Ben and Zoe stood in stunned silence. They hadn't thought Mr. Ostriander would commit murder to get his hands on the reservation.

At that moment, an ear-splitting chirping noise filled the air. Zoe saw Ben's BUG drop to the ground, and she saw the slight move of his foot as he kicked it under a bush.

Mr. Ostriander jumped in shock at hearing the loud call. He pulled a gun out from his pocket. "What's that noise?" he asked.

"Must be a bird," said Ben, trying to keep his breathing calm. "It's probably scared of the four-wheeler."

Mr. Ostriander lowered his gun. "You should thank me, really," he said with a cold smile. "You're going to be famous! It will be in all the papers tomorrow that Mat and two young tourists were killed in a tragic ballooning accident." Mr. Ostriander let out a harsh chuckle. "Of course," he said, "you won't be alive to see it."

"You can't just kill us," Zoe said. "Someone will figure out what you did!"

"Everyone will fall for it, Zoe," Mr. Ostriander said. "And there'll be no evidence left behind because a forest fire is going to sweep through the entire reservation."

"I thought you were a friend, Peter," Mat whispered. "To me, to the local people, and to the animals on this reservation."

Ostriander laughed as he turned back to his four-wheeler. He pulled out a long coil of rope.

Zoe began to back away. Mr. Ostriander raised an eyebrow. "Stay still, Zoe," he warned. "I would prefer not to shoot you, as bullets will survive the fire. But I will if I have to."

"But if you start a fire," Zoe said desperately, "it might burn your oil palms,"

"I have thought of that, Zoe," said Mr. Ostriander. "The wind's not heading in that direction. Talib and I checked that carefully." He looked at his watch. "In fact, he should be starting the fire now."

There was a sudden shriek above all of their heads. Mr. Ostriander looked up in horror to see a furious blur of orange fur hurling itself right at him.

"It's Kawan!" yelled Zoe.

With astonishing speed, the orangutan crashed into Mr. Ostriander and sent him sprawling. The gun flew out of his hands and landed nearby.

Kawan curled his lips in a snarl and bent over to pick up the weapon. "Get rid of it, Kawan," Mat said gently. "Throw it away."

With a sharp cry, Kawan raised the gun high over his head. He tossed the weapon. It disappeared into the undergrowth.

Next, Kawan lurched toward Mr. Ostriander. Terrified, he scrambled to his feet and stumbled toward his four-wheeler. Kawan stopped and watched him roar away.

Kawan threw back his head and let out a loud call. Creatures all around took up the cry.

For a few seconds, the canopy was alive with harsh howls and squawks. Then the orangutan turned back to stare at Ben and Zoe. Kawan showed no sign of anger now. He squatted next to Mat, stroking his head.

Mat smiled at his friend. "Good boy," he said in a faint whisper. "Brave boy."

"We need to get out of here before Talib starts the fire," said Zoe. She went up to Mat and slipped her hand underneath his arm.

Ben reached for his BUG. Uncle Stephen needed to know the danger they were in. He was just pressing the WILD hot key when he heard a frightened shout.

"Ben," said Zoe. "I can smell smoke. The fire's coming!"

CHAPTER 12

HEAT

"Hello!" came Uncle Stephen's voice.

"Ostriander's trying to sabotage the reservation!" Ben yelled into the BUG. "He's burning the forest — with us in it!"

"I've found your position using your signal," Uncle Stephen's voice said. "The fire's west of you. Head east — as fast as you can!"

Lifting him by the arm, Zoe helped Mat to his feet. "You're coming with us!" she said.

Mat painfully staggered a few paces, then swayed and leaned heavily on her shoulder. Ben came and supported Mat's other side.

Kawan gave a low, anxious cry and waddled away. Then he stopped, turned, and chattered at them urgently. Ben checked the map on his BUG. "I think Kawan's heading for the plantation," he said. "And it looks like he wants us to follow him."

Zoe nodded. They moved as fast as they could, half-carrying Mat between them. Roots and vines threatened to trip them with every step. Above their heads, they could see wind disturbing the tops of the trees. It was blowing toward them as they ran.

"At least the wind's not blowing the fire our way," Zoe said through gritted teeth.

Then the burning smell suddenly grew stronger. They tasted smoke on their tongues. Ben and Zoe took shallow breaths to prevent themselves from choking. They could hear Mat's gasps for air as he forced himself forward. The trees above were filled with alarmed cries and scrabbling noises of animals as they fled their homes. Kawan urged them on with loud calls.

"Uh-oh," said Zoe. "The wind changed direction."

Zoe fell forward as her foot got caught in a thick exposed root. She landed in the middle of a brightly colored plant. The fleshy leaves parted, showering her with water and insects. Mat fell to his knees, but Ben was able to keep him upright. He helped Zoe to her feet with his other hand.

"Can you feel how hot it's getting?" Zoe asked.

Zoe turned to look behind her. Her eyes went wide and she raised her shaky finger, pointing at an orange light flickering in the distance. "The fire's coming this way!" she said in a horrified whisper.

They lurched onward as fast as they could, following Kawan. CRACK! A terrible sound filled the smoky air. CRACK! Another noise rang out.

"The trees are exploding!" yelled Ben. "We have to move faster."

The black smoke was making it almost impossible to catch their breath. Sweat poured into their eyes, blinding them. Ben wiped his hand across his face. Behind them, the flames were licking at the canopy of trees. Kawan stopped as they came to the edge of the plantation.

The regularly spaced oil palm trees were just ahead. Kawan turned and chattered anxiously, urging them forward. Mat pulled back. "Can't go that way," he said weakly. "Oil palms burn very fast!"

"We don't have a choice," Ben said, pulling Mat along a corridor of trees. "There's no way back."

Trees and shrubs were becoming engulfed in a relentless wave of flame. Red-hot embers showered down on them, stinging their skin like vicious wasps. Zoe and Ben brushed the embers from their clothes. Kawan was giving frightened little cries as the sparks fell on to his fur.

Zoe's mouth was full of ash. The heat made her lungs ache. She glanced at Ben's soot-streaked face. He was doing no better. Mat was barely able to shuffle along now.

Zoe knew they couldn't stop. The fire had reached the oil palms. The trees were devoured by flames faster than she could believe.

As they pushed their way through the undergrowth, Mat collapsed to the ground. The children tried to pull him back to his feet, but he wasn't moving. Kawan came to his side, whining softly.

"We have to keep going," cried Zoe, her voice cracking. "We'll be burned alive!"

"Leave me," Mat whispered. "I can't go any farther."

Then, all of a sudden, Ben felt something wet hit his hand. He looked up. All he could see was a swirl of thick, dark smoke. But through that smoke, drops of water fell on his face.

Ben grabbed Zoe's arm. He shook it to get her attention. "Look!" he whispered.

Zoe lifted her face toward the sky. Soft wet drops splashed against her face. "It's raining!" she cried.

CHAPTER 13

RELIEF

The next morning was bright and sunny. The smell of yesterday's fire still hung in the air, but the smoke was gone. Bird and monkey cries could be heard in the canopy once again. Ben and Zoe stood on the walkway, looking out at Kawan's territory.

Ben grinned. "Listen to that racket," he said. "It's as if nothing even happened."

"It's amazing that this part of the reservation was spared from the flames," said Zoe.

"If that rainstorm hadn't come when it did . . ." Zoe trailed off. She looked down at her bandaged hands. The burns were painful, but it could have been a lot worse.

Just then, Zoe's BUG beeped. She pulled it out and read the incoming text. "Erika says she'll be coming to get us this afternoon," she told Ben.

"It's a shame we can't stay to help Mat," he said. "He has so much extra work to do now. He's lost about half of his trees."

"Did I hear my name?" came a voice from behind them. They turned to see Mat slowly making his way along the rope walkway. Yasmin, with Biza hanging from her shoulders, followed behind.

"He must have finished talking with the police," whispered Zoe. The police had questioned the children first.

Ben and Zoe told them they were frightened tourists, which wasn't a lie at all. But they were also able to give a lot of details about Mr. Ostriander's crimes.

"I brought some cookies," Mat said cheerfully. He steadied himself on the rope handrail. Like Ben and Zoe, he had burns on his hands. "This little troublemaker has been trying to steal them all day!" He carefully pulled the bag out of his pocket and gave one to little Biza.

"Any sign of Kawan?" asked Yasmin.

Ben and Zoe shook their heads sadly.

"Kawan's a hero now," said Mat. "We've had telephone calls from television and radio stations all over the world asking to hear about the amazing rescue and how he led us away from the fire."

"And the best part is," added Yasmin, "everyone's all right. And it's gotten us a lot of publicity. We've had people getting in contact wanting to know how they can help support the reservation. A company in Japan wants to sponsor us, and we've had students from colleges all over the world asking to volunteer their time here."

Zoe frowned. "But you've also lost a lot of trees," she said.

"That's true," said Mat. "But within a week, there will be new ones starting to spring up. There are many dormant seeds lying quietly under the cover of the other trees that have been waiting for the chance to sprout. It will take some time, but it will eventually grow back."

"Do you think the animals are safe?" asked Ben.

Mat nodded. "They're much better than we are at sensing danger," he said.

"And the police have put out a warrant for Peter's arrest already," Yasmin said. "Although how they were able to do it so fast is a mystery."

Ben and Zoe caught each other's eye but made sure not to smile. They knew that, once again, Uncle Stephen had gotten his messages through to the right people.

"Talib confessed everything," Mat said soberly. "Once they catch Mr. Ostriander, the case will be closed!"

A knowing smile covered Mat's face as he looked down at Ben and Zoe. "When I was hurt," he said, "I thought I heard you call Kawan with some little device."

Ben and Zoe glanced at each other.

Zoe grinned. "You must have just been delirious," she said kindly. "You'd been knocked out in that balloon, after all."

Mat smiled. "Of course," he said with a wink. "How ridiculous of me!"

He put his hands on their shoulders. Tears were welling in the corner of his eyes. "In any case," he said, "you two are heroes. I owe you my life. Thank you, from the bottom of my heart."

Ben and Zoe smiled shyly up at Mat. Just then, the branches in a nearby tree swished and Kawan appeared.

"There's the real hero!" Zoe said, pointing at Kawan. She tried to make the chirping noise that Mat showed them, but it sounded more like a squawk.

"Let me try!" Ben said. He rolled his tongue and made a clicking sound.

Kawan immediately responded and lumbered toward them. "Impressive!" Mat said to Ben. "You only heard it once or twice, yet you were able to copy it very well."

Kawan sat down in front of them with his head cocked to the side. Mat handed the paper bag to Zoe. "I think he's waiting for something," Mat said with a grin.

Zoe removed a biscuit and held it out. With a low purring sound, Kawan reached out a long arm and took it in his fingers. He sniffed it for a moment, and then began to nibble at the edges.

Ben laughed. "He's being very polite!" he said.

Kawan stared at Zoe as he ate. Then he froze, his eyes glued to something over her shoulder.

Kawan pulled back his lips and let out a howl that made Ben and Zoe jump. A loud chattering began behind them. They turned to see Biza waving his hands above his head excitedly.

Ben grinned. "I think Kawan's saying hello to Biza!" he said.

"I think he's saying something to us all," said Zoe.

"What's that?" asked Mat.

Zoe smiled. "It's obvious," she said. "He's saying, 'I'm home.'"

THE AUTHORS

Jan Burchett and **Sara Vogler** were already friends when they discovered they both wanted to write children's books, and that it was much more fun to do it together. They have since written over a hundred and thirty stories ranging from educational books and stories for younger readers to young adult fiction. They have written for series such as Dinosaur Cove and Beast Quest, and they are authors of the Gargoylz books.

THE ILLUSTRATOR

Diane Le Feyer discovered a passion for drawing and animation at the age of five. In 2002, she graduated with honors from the Ecole Emile Cohl school of design. Diane worked as a character designer, 3D modeler, and animator in the video games industry before joining the Cartoon Saloon animation studio, where she worked as a director, animator, illustrator, and character designer. Diane was also a part of the early design and development of the movie *The Secret of Kells*.

GLOSSARY

Borneo (BOR-nee-oh)—an island in the Malay archipelago

canopy (KAN-uh-pee)—the ledge of trees that hangs over the rainforest

endangered (en-DAYN-jurd)—at risk of going extinct

intel (IN-tel)—information

mission (MISH-uhn)—a special job or task

operative (OP-ur-uh-tiv)—a secret agent

plantation (plan-TAY-shuhn)—a large farm found in warm climates where crops such as coffee, tea, rubber, and cotton are grown

rainforest (RAYN-for-ist)—a dense, tropical forest where a lot of rain falls

reservation (rez-ur-VAY-shuhn)—an area of land set aside by the government to be preserved for a special purpose

sanctuary (SANGK-choo-er-ee)—a natural area where animals are protected from hunters

urgent (UR-juhnt)—if something is urgent, it needs quick or immediate attention

THE ORANGUTAN
STATUS: ENDANGERED

Orangutans are found on the islands of Borneo and Sumatra. In 1900, there were approximately 315,000 orangutans living in the wild. Now there are only about 60,000. Several threats have contributed to their dwindling numbers.

LOSS OF HABITAT: In the last 20 years, orangutans have lost over 80 percent of their habitat. Tropical rainforests are being cut down for timber, and the land is being cleared for use as oil palm plantations and for mining. Forest fires also threaten orangutans' homes.

EXTERMINATION: Orangutans are sometimes killed for interfering with plantation operations by owners and farmers.

LOW REPRODUCTION: In the wild, a female orangutan only gives birth every seven to eight years, with an average of four surviving offspring over her entire lifespan.

PREDATORS: Humans, clouded leopards, tigers, and several other predators are all threats to the orangutan.

ILLEGAL PET TRADE: In some areas, mother orangutans are killed after giving birth so their babies can be sold as pets.

BUT THERE'S STILL HOPE FOR THE ORANGUTAN! In 2009, scientists discovered a large population of around 2,000 orangutans in the remote jungles of Borneo. Conservationists are hard at work trying to preserve and protect the area so the local apes can live happily and increase their numbers.

DISCUSSION QUESTIONS

1. Ben and Zoe are twins. Do you have any siblings? Do you think it would be good to have a twin? Talk about brothers and sisters.

2. Out of all the things Zoe and Ben do in this book, which was the most exciting? Talk about their adventures.

3. There are many illustrations in this book. Which one is your favorite? Why?

WRITING PROMPTS

1. Mr. Ostriander is this book's villain. Write a story about a hero that battles a villain. What does your villain look like? What is his or her name? Who wins? Write about a battle between a villain and a hero.

2. Mat trains Kawan to perform tricks and obey commands. If you had to take care of an orangutan, what kinds of things would you teach it? Write about your exotic pet.

3. The orangutan in this book helps Zoe and Ben escape a forest fire. Imagine that you were trapped in a forest fire. How would you escape? Who — or what — would help you escape? Write about it.